Bella Basset Ballerina

In memory of my mother, Doris Duenewald Garn,
and for my daughters, Louisa and Emma Thanhauser. — L.A.G.

To my beloved daughter, Nikkie. — V.S.

Text copyright 2001 by Laura Aimee Garn
Illustrations copyright 2004 by Valerie Sokolova
Designer: Jacqueline Kachman, Kachman Design
The text of this book is set in 12 pt. Goudy
The illustrations are rendered in gouache with airbrush.
Endpaper paw prints by Gaston of New York City

Pretty Please Press, Inc. 105 East 29th Street, 6th Floor New York, New York 10016
First Edition
10 9 8 7 6 5 4 3 2 1
Printed in U.S.A.

Library of Congress Control Number: 2004195155
ISBN Hardcover: 0-9759378-0-4
ISBN Paperback edition: 0-9759378-5-5

On a beautiful fall afternoon in Bowserburg, Bella Basset
scampered home from school. She nipped at the leaves that swirled
through the air and bounded through crunchy leaf piles by the road.

She played "Steal the Bacon" with her twin brothers, Beau
and Bart, and helped them practice their fetching.

Bella and her mother set the table with chow and kibble, and the Basset family sat down to dinner.

"I've thought of a treat for Bella's birthday," Mrs. Basset announced. "I'm going to take her to Fideaux Falls to see the Royal Borzoi Ballet Company. Would anyone else like to come?"

Mr. Basset's jowls drooped. "Wish I could go, Bertha, but I have to work on the woodchucks and chase the moles."

"We'd rather play with the Dachshunds," said Bart.

"But we'll still have birthday cake, won't we?" asked Beau.

"Of course," Mrs. Basset winked at Bella. "Bella and I will go to the ballet, and we'll have birthday cake when we come home."

5

Bella's celebration began with lunch at an elegant cafe.

"The fountain, the fancy Poodles — it's all so grand!" Bella exclaimed as she and her mother shared a delicious kidney and giblet pudding. Bella pointed out an imperious Chinese Crested, hopping from a car across the town square.

"She's going to Zsa Zsa's Salon, the most exclusive grooming shop,"
said Mrs. Basset. "Maybe we'll go there someday!"
After lunch, Bella and her mother hurried to the Opera House.

Bella panted with excitement as the dancers waltzed onto the stage. The prima ballerina, Mademoiselle Ada, had long hair that rippled when she danced.

"I want to be just like Mademoiselle Ada when I grow up," Bella said.

"That's a sweet idea, Bella," said her mother. "But every dog is born with a way to live and a job to do. We Bassets are short, and we have stubby legs. Our stomachs scrape the ground. We are suited to country life. Borzois are tall and graceful. They are meant to dance."

"You mean I'm supposed to stay on the farm, chasing and digging?" said Bella.

"Of course. The farm is where you belong."

I may be low to the ground, and I may belong on the farm, but I'm going to dance, thought Bella.

That night, snuggled in her bed, Bella dreamed of leaps and twirls, of fluffy tutus and elegant pink slippers.

The next day she ran out to the field and tried to leap in the air the way Mademoiselle Ada had done. Bella landed hard. She tried again and she tripped, rolled forward, and bruised her nose on a rock. She jumped in the air again and again, until she finally landed with a spring in her step.

On Saturday, Bella took the bus to Fideaux Falls and waited by the stage door until she saw the prima ballerina. The graceful Ada peered through sweeping eyelashes at her eager fan.

"I saw the ballet last week," said Bella. "And I want to dance."

"Ah, yes," said Ada. "Ballet is beautiful. But you are a country dog, and ballet is not for you. Each dog to his own path — that is the way of our world."

With that Ada disappeared, leaving only a cloud of L'Air du Chien perfume.

Bella was snuffling with disappointment when a Wolfhound opened the door.

"I am Madame Petrovna, wardrobe mistress," she said. "Can I help you, my dear?"

Bella told Madame about the magical day when she first saw the ballet, her practice in the field, and her talk with Mademoiselle Ada.

"It's true that you are on the short side," said Madame Petrovna. "In our world it would be impossible for you to dance. We are, after all, the Royal Borzoi Ballet. But I know of a place where animals can do what they want to do. It's called the Big City."

"There I could be a ballerina?" said Bella.

"First you must find someone willing to teach you."

"And then I'll be a ballerina?"

"Not quite. You will work and sacrifice. You may try, fail, and try again. But someday you might do the work you love."

"Do you think I can do it?"

"You must try." Madame Petrovna studied Bella. "Your tail has a nice arc. Go to Monsieur Boris on Pointer Road. Tell him that Madame Petrovna sent you to dance, dance, dance."

"Thank you, Madame Petrovna," said Bella. "Thank you so much."

Bella found Monsieur Boris's studio and approached the great teacher. "Monsieur Boris, I'm here to dance," she said.

"You're very… earthbound, my little Basset," he said. "Excuse me. I'm about to teach a class."

"Please, Monsieur, I know I can learn."

"Bassets aren't meant to dance, my dear," Monsieur Boris said gently. "They burrow and lope, and sometimes dash, but they do not dance."

14

"Let me show you what I can do," said Bella.

"You are very persistent," sighed Monsieur Boris.

Bella ran, sprang into a leap, and landed firmly on all fours.

"You do have talent," Monsieur Boris said. He studied her for a moment. "I will take you on as a private student."

"I promise to work hard!" said Bella, looking around the room at the pictures of famous Borzoi ballerinas in sparkling costumes. "I am going to be a dancer."

That night Bella told her parents that she was going to study
ballet in Fideaux Falls with Monsieur Boris, the famous ballet master.

"But you can't dance — you're a Basset," said Bella's mother.
"Bertram, are you going to put your paw down?"

"No," said her father. "If Bella has found a teacher, we can't stand
in her way. Dancing will strengthen her legs, so she'll run and dig faster.
Failure builds character. Ballet will make her a better Basset."

And so Bella's dream — and a life of sacrifice — began. Bella did
her chores before school, and went to Fideaux Falls for her class with
Monsieur Boris in the afternoon.

He taught her all the ballet positions — the demi and grand
pliés, the turns, the jumps, the leaps. Dancing was hard work, but Bella
loved it.

After a few months, Bella joined the advanced class. The other
dancers, silky Borzois, tittered when they saw her. But as Bella began to
dance, the Borzois watched, stunned.

"Beautiful!" said Monsieur Boris. "You are ready to go to the Big
City. And you will come back a star!"

When she arrived in the Big City, Bella was dazzled by the enormous buildings, the streets, the signs, the lights... and the citizens! She had never seen such huge creatures.

"Move your trunk!" a zebra brayed to an elephant in the intersection.

Bella approached a rhinoceros who was directing traffic.

"Excuse me, sir," she said, trying to be heard above all the snorting and bleating. "Do you know where I can find the ballet?"

"Ballet? What's that?" bellowed the rhino.

"Dancing, you big lug," said a little bird who was sitting on the rhino's shoulder. "Go to the Hippodrome on the Grand Plaza, Puppy. Everything's there — theater, music, ballet. You're in the Big City now!"

Bella trotted through the legs of the large creatures crowding the avenues and made her way to the Hippodrome. Finally she was standing beneath a tree filled with parrots.

"I'm here to audition for the Big City Ballet," said Bella.

"Check the board; check the board," squawked a parrot.

There were two other dogs reading the list of shows holding auditions. "No one is looking for a dancing dog today," the Spaniel sighed.

"Don't give up, don't give up," said one bird.

"Get a day job, get a day job," screeched another.

"What can I do?" asked Bella. Then she noticed a dog who was leading a herd of sheep. The dog was speaking with authority.

"Built in ancient times by Hippo the Fourth, known as 'Hippo the Hefty,' the Hippodrome was the first center of entertainment in the Big City," said the dog. The sheep followed their guide, bleating with interest.

"Be a Big City tour guide, Puppy," the parrot squawked.

Bella found a comfortable room in a boarding house, where she made new friends. There was Claudio, a cheetah who aspired to sing in the opera. There was Gloria, a giraffe who designed sets for the theater, and Leopold, a lemur who worked as a trapeze artist in the circus.

Bella led tours in the morning and took ballet classes in the afternoon with all kinds of dancers — gazelles, camels, even rhinos and hippos. It was just as Madame Petrovna had told her: Anyone could dance in the Big City.

Every day Bella went to the Hippodrome to check the casting board. Sometimes she went to auditions. She almost got a role in "Waltz for a Weasel," and she was called back twice for the "Tapir Tarantella." But there was never a part for her.

She looked forward to her weekly letter from her parents, with paw prints from Bart and Beau. Sometimes Bella was so homesick that she loped down to the bus station to watch the buses going to Bowserburg.

One day Bella saw a sign on the casting board: *Dancers Wanted,
Canine Carnival, Stage Six.* Canine — this could be her big chance!
Bella raced up the stairs. She was so excited that she didn't stop to change
in the dressing room or to warm up. She bounded right onto the stage.
Bella remembered everything that Monsieur Boris had taught her. She
pressed her haunches to the floor, raised her ears, and sprang up as
high as she could.

Her tail arched beautifully. She could see the ballet master, an oryx, nodding with pleasure.

"Wonderful! What do you think?" he asked the director.

"I have never seen a dog leap so high," the director exclaimed, turning to the producer.

"This Basset is fabulous," the producer cried. "My dear, we have a place for you in our production!"

Bella made her debut in the Big City Ballet Company.
Her pirouettes were precise, and she soared as high as the gazelles.
Bella was featured in the "Sirloin Sonata," a lyrical piece.

The Big City critics hailed Bella as an overnight sensation, noting
her agility and her dazzling technique.

After Bella's great success in the Big City, the ballet company travelled to the Opera House in Fideaux Falls. Bella's family, along with Monsieur Boris, came to see her.

"You are truly a ballerina, Bella," said her mother after the performance.

"We're proud of your dancing," said her father. "And proud that you went to the Big City all by yourself."

"Ballet isn't boring, after all," said Beau.

"Even if it's not as much fun as basketball," said Bart.

Later, when a reporter was interviewing Bella, Mademoiselle Ada worked her way to the front of the crowd.

"I spotted Bella's talent from the beginning," she declared, batting her long eyelashes at the reporter.

"Mademoiselle Ada may have spotted my talent, but Monsieur Boris gave me a chance to dance," said Bella. "I owe my success to his encouragement."

"Bella owes her success to her own persistence," said Boris.

Bella continued her career as a rising star of the Big City Ballet Company, but she always found time in her busy schedule to return to Fideaux Falls to teach at Monsieur Boris's studio.

In Bella's honor, Boris established a master class for "Aspiring Dancers of Unusual Breeds." Bella encouraged her star pupils, Wilhemina, Binky, and Dorie, to go to the Big City and audition as she had done.

For Bella's contribution to Fideaux Falls, Mayor Pugsley awarded her the Gold Key to the Kennels. As she accepted the honor, Bella spoke to an admiring crowd: "I believe that every dog has a way to live and a job to do, which only he or she should choose. Every dog has his day, darlings! And every dog can dance!"